D1442006

Short "a"
and Long "a"
Play a Game

Library of Congress Cataloging-in-Publication Data
Moncure, Jane Belk.
Short "a" and long "a" play a game / by Jane Belk Moncure ; illustrated by Norman Young.
p. cm.
Summary: Short a and Long a introduce the long and short "a" sounds.
ISBN 1-56766-928-X (library bound)
[1. English language—Vowels—Fiction.]   I. Young, N. (Norman), ill. II. Title.
PZ7.M739 Sf 2001
[E]—dc21
00-010848

Short "a"
and Long "a"
Play a Game

Jane Belk Moncure

illustrated by Norman Young

This is . He has a special sound.

Alligator

begins with his short "a" sound.

So does 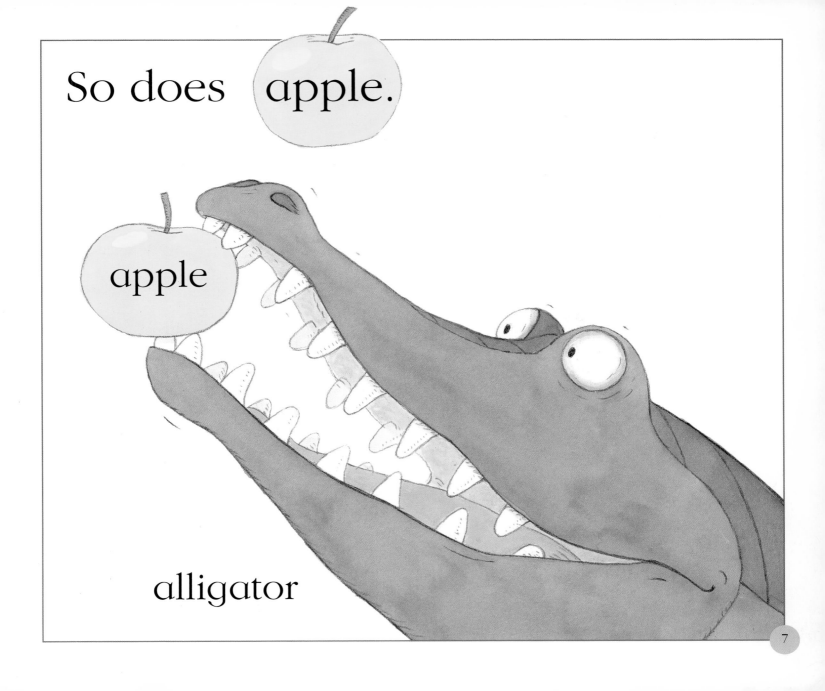 apple.

apple

alligator

This is  long a . She has a different sound.

Ape begins with her long "a" sound.

8

So does apron.

apron

 ape

Can you hear the

and the sounds?

apple

alligator

One day,
Short "a" said,
"Let's play a game.
I will look for my sound in words.

ape

apron

You can look for your sound in words. We'll see who can find the most words."

Short **a** found an arrow,

an ax,

an ant,

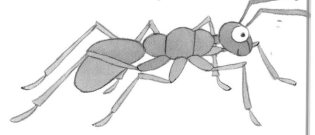

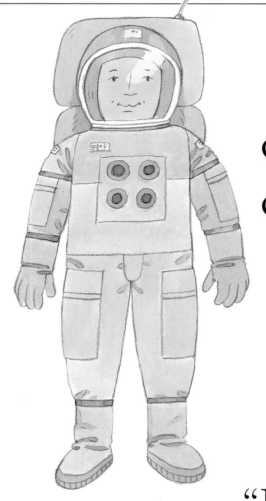

and an
astronaut.

"I will win!"  said.

Long **a** found acorns...

and an angel.

"No! I will win!"
she said.

astronaut

ax

ant

alligator

apple

arrow

Short **a**

counted. "I win," he said.
"I have the most words."

apron

acorns

ape

angel

Long a counted.

"No! No! No!" she said.

"I will use my  eyes

and 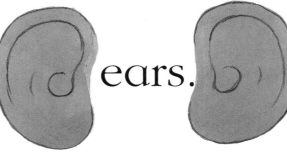 ears.

My sound hides in words.
I will find words with
my sound in the middle
of them."

Long **a** found...

a rake,

a cake,

a lake,

and a snake.

Then  a found a cape

for the ape

and grapes

for the ape.

"Now I will win!" said 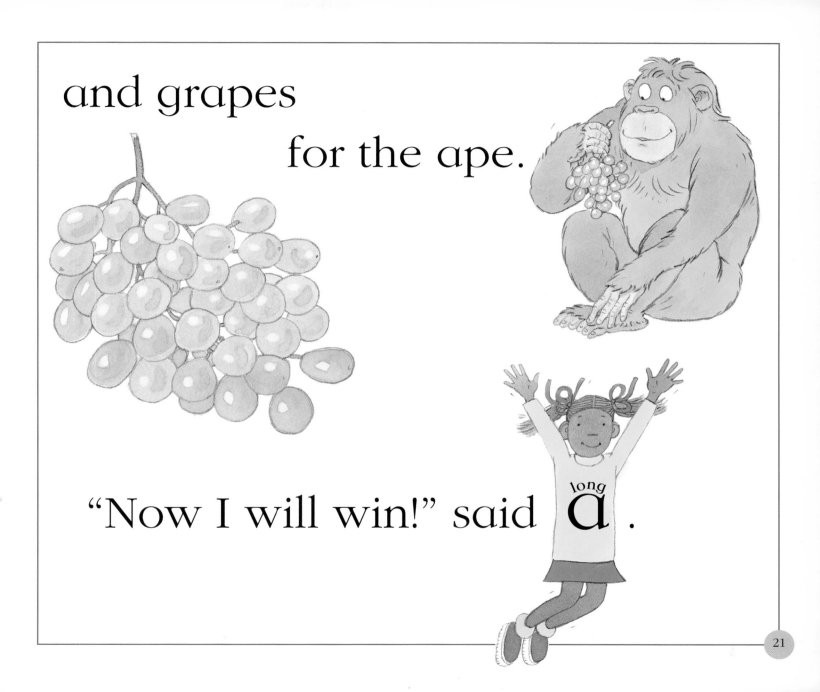.

"No! No! No!" said  .

"I will use my eyes

and 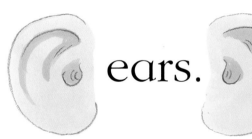 ears.

My sound hides in words, too.
I will find words with my sound
in the middle of them."

Short **a** found a camel,

a cat,

a bat,

and a rat.

23

Then  found rabbits

and radishes

for the rabbits.

"Now I win!" said  .

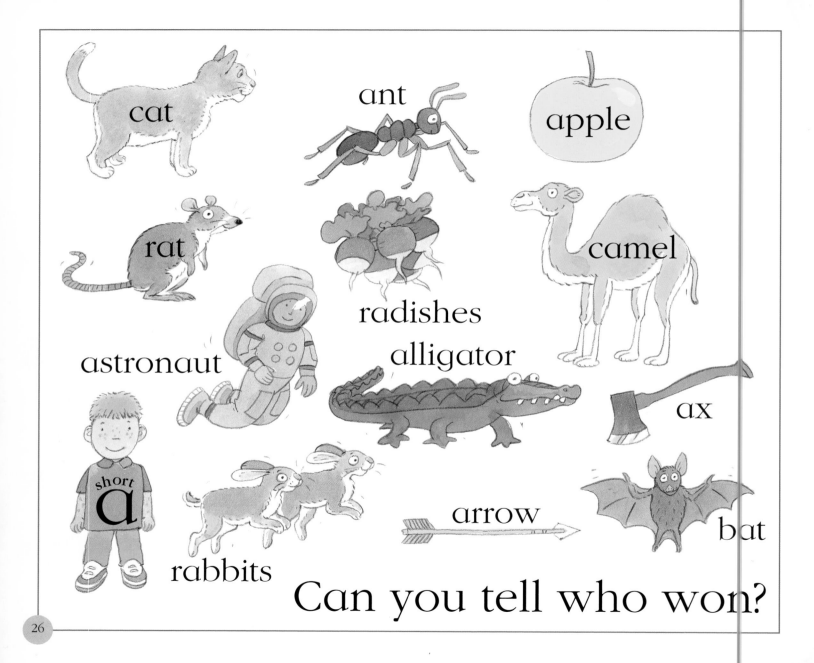

cat

ant

apple

rat

radishes

camel

astronaut

alligator

ax

short a

rabbits

arrow

bat

Can you tell who won?

lake

cake

cape

grapes

apron

angel

rake

ape

snake

acorns

long a

Can you read more words with 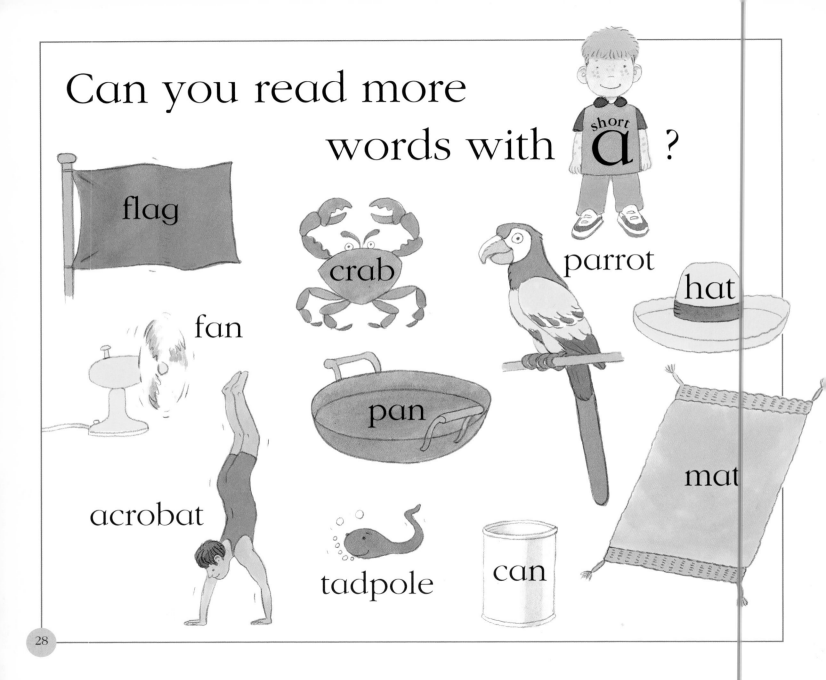 short **a**?

flag

crab

parrot

hat

fan

pan

mat

acrobat

tadpole

can

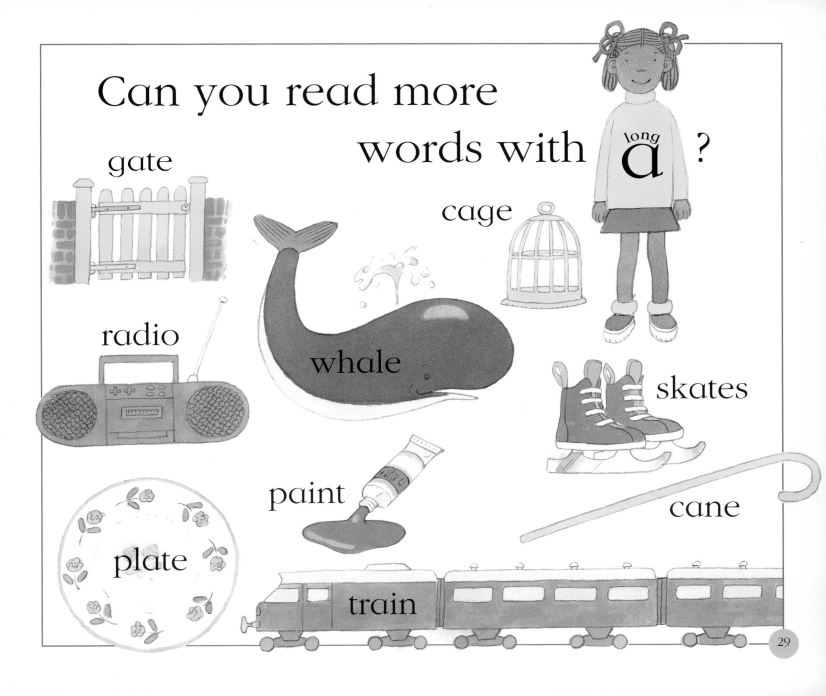

Can you read more words with long a ?

gate

cage

radio

whale

skates

paint

cane

plate

train

29

Now you make up a game!

ABOUT THE AUTHOR AND ILLUSTRATOR

Jane Belk Moncure began her writing career when she was in kindergarten. She has never stopped writing. Many of her children's stories and poems have been published, to the delight of young readers, including her son Jim, whose childhood experiences found their way into many of her books.

Mrs. Moncure's writing is based upon an active career in early childhood education. A recipient of an M.A. degree from Columbia University, Mrs. Moncure has taught and directed nursery, kindergarten, and primary grade programs in California, New York, Virginia, and North Carolina. As a former member of the faculties of Virginia Commonwealth University and the University of Richmond, she taught prospective teachers in early childhood education.

Mrs. Moncure has travelled extensively abroad, studying early childhood programs in the United Kingdom, The Netherlands, and Switzerland. She was the first president of the Virginia Association for Early Childhood Education and received its award for outstanding service to young children. A resident of North Carolina, Mrs. Moncure is currently a full-time writer and educational consultant. She is married to Dr. James A. Moncure, former vice president of Elon College.

Norman Young spent his childhood on a small farm nestled at the foot of the Preseli Hills in Pembrokeshire, South West Wales. He started his artistic career as a film animator in London and then in Zagreb. Eventually he settled in Devon, where he lives beside a river that runs between the moors and the sea. It was here that he started his work as an illustrator of children's books. Norman has always had a lifelong interest in history and travel. Taking a month off work each year, he visits new places either by train or by bicycle—and he never goes anywhere without his sketchbook.